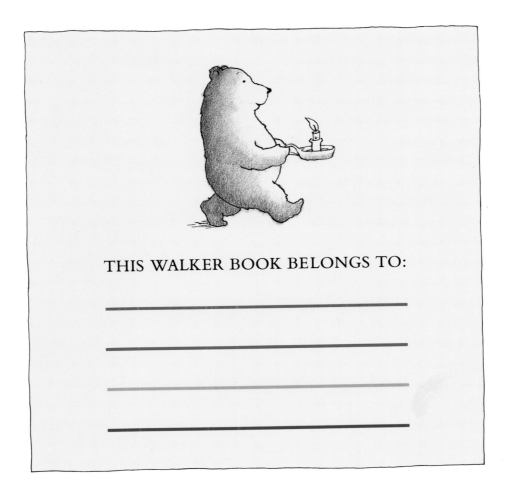

THIS WALKER BOOK BELONGS TO:

_____

_____

_____

_____

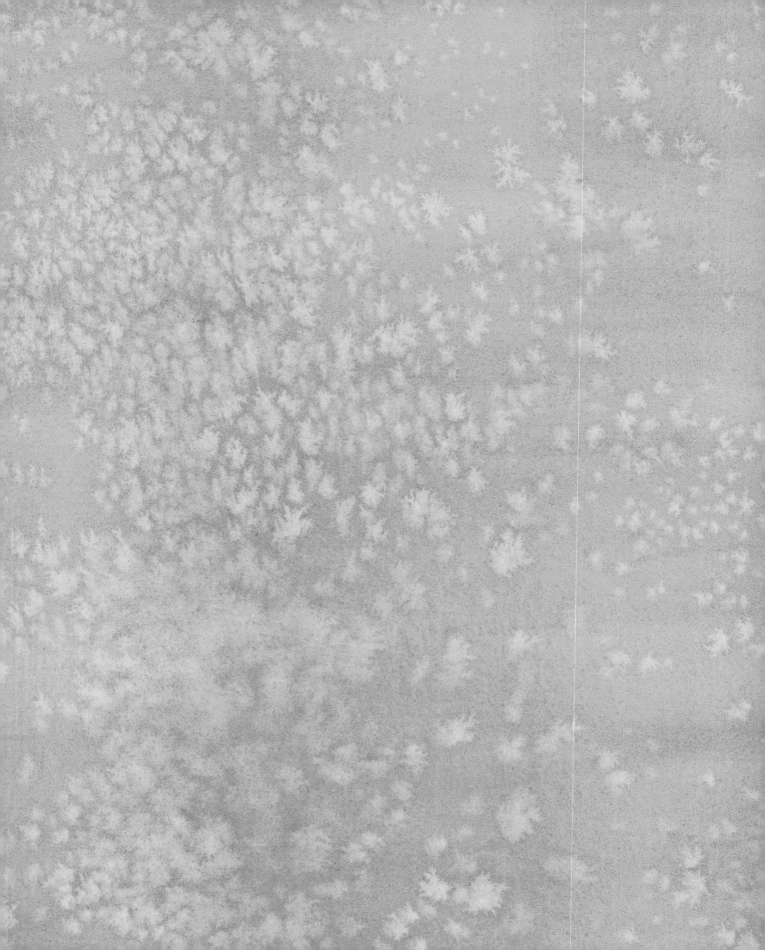

For D.B.

First published 1990 by Walker Books Ltd
87 Vauxhall Walk, London SE11 5HJ

Text © 1990 Anne Carter
Illustrations © 1990 Louise Brierley

This edition published 1993

Printed and bound in Hong Kong by
South China Printing Co. (1988) Ltd

British Library Cataloguing in Publication Data
A catalogue record for this book is
available from the British Library.
ISBN 0-7445-3076-8

THE FISHERWOMAN

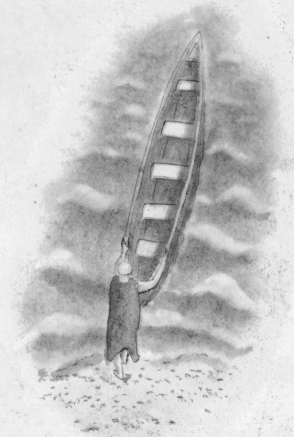

Louise Brierley

Words by

Anne Carter

WALKER BOOKS
LONDON

In a small, shabby village beside the sea,
lived Maud, the fisherwoman. By day,
she combed the shore for shells and sea-wrack. As
the sun set, she rowed her long, lean boat out over
the water and let down her fishing net. And this was
how she made her living.

But, sitting alone, while her boat rocked gently
under her, Maud dreamed. Her dream was always the
same: dressed in beautiful clothes, she moved among
the rich and famous people who lived behind the
great gates of the mansion above the village.

One night, when the time came to draw in her net, Maud felt a hard bump against the side of the boat. Her head filled with visions of sunken treasure, jewels, perhaps, worth more than a king's ransom. But when she hauled the net aboard, all she found, among the flapping bream and mackerel, was an old pink vase.

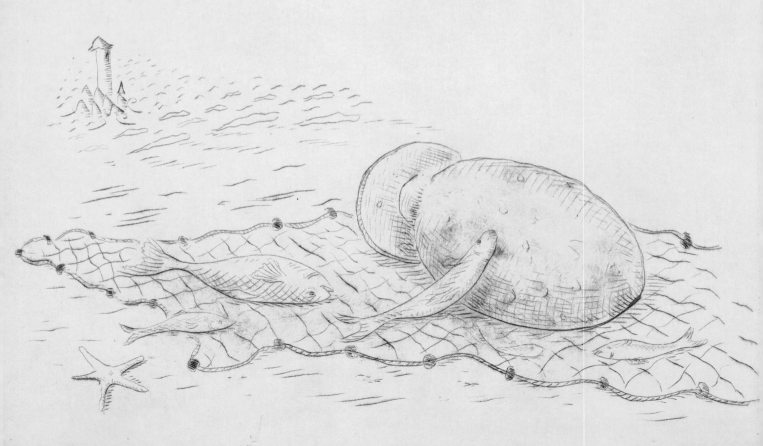

Maud took the vase home with her and
put it in her window. Now and then, as she
sat at her table, her eyes would rest on it and
fancy that they saw, on its sea-incrusted sides,
shadowy figures moving in a kind of dance.
But time passed, bringing other curious
trophies from the sea and Maud lost
interest in the vase.

With autumn came high winds and seas too fierce for fishing. Maud lay in bed, but not asleep. Outside, the storm raged and the rain lashed her house. Soon, beneath the turmoil, came a sullen dripping. Sighing, Maud got up and began putting out every pot and jar she had to catch the water. Among them was the old pink vase. The hollow drips became a musical splashing and Maud slept.

The storm blew itself out and a red dawn gave way to quiet sunshine. Out of Maud's pink vase grew a tall rubbery stem with, at the very top, a single large pink flower bud. It was the first thing she saw when she awoke.

While she watched, the bud expanded into a wild, beautiful, shell-like flower. Maud was entranced. She moved the vase into a sunny corner and gazed at the flower for a long, long time.

She spent the rest of that day gathering shellfish off the rocks and picking up storm wreckage from the beach. When she came home, she saw that the petals of the pink flower had fallen and, in their place, as if the tree had fruited, was the most incredible pink hat.

Maud picked it. It came quite readily into her hand. She hurried to her looking-glass and tried it on.

Next morning, Maud's wonder grew. The
plant had borne two more fruits in the shape of a pair
of marvellous pink shoes.

Maud leapt out of bed and put them on.
They fitted perfectly. She wanted the whole world
to see. She went out, without pausing for breakfast,
parading up the village street to show off her finery.
People greeted her and Maud smiled graciously
but did not speak.

On the third morning, Maud woke very early. She was not disappointed. The tree had fruited again, still more magnificently. This time it bore a pink dress, the most beautiful thing that Maud had ever seen. It fitted as if it had been made for her.

Maud hurried out to show herself. She held her head so high that she did not even see the friends who greeted her. Or the grins that followed her up the street.

She was strolling along the promenade when the Contessa came by in her gondola.

"Dear madam, will you join us at my mansion? The garden party is about to begin."

And so, to the lap-lapping of the water and the chat-chatting of the lady, Maud was borne across the bay.

Inside the high walls, the music and the fountains played. People talked and laughed and such a banquet was laid out as Maud had never in her life imagined. All day she revelled in wealth and splendour, thinking of nothing but the pleasure of it all. Long shadows crept across the lawns and still the guests sat eating and drinking.

The late sun
gilded the great gates
and Maud could see
the villagers passing
by outside. A fat man
sitting next to her
was mocking them.
Maud looked around
her, saw the greedy
faces, heard the
heartless laughter,
and suddenly she
knew how selfish she
had been. She did not
belong here, sealed
behind these iron
gates. Her place was
in the real world,
doing the work she
knew, among friends.

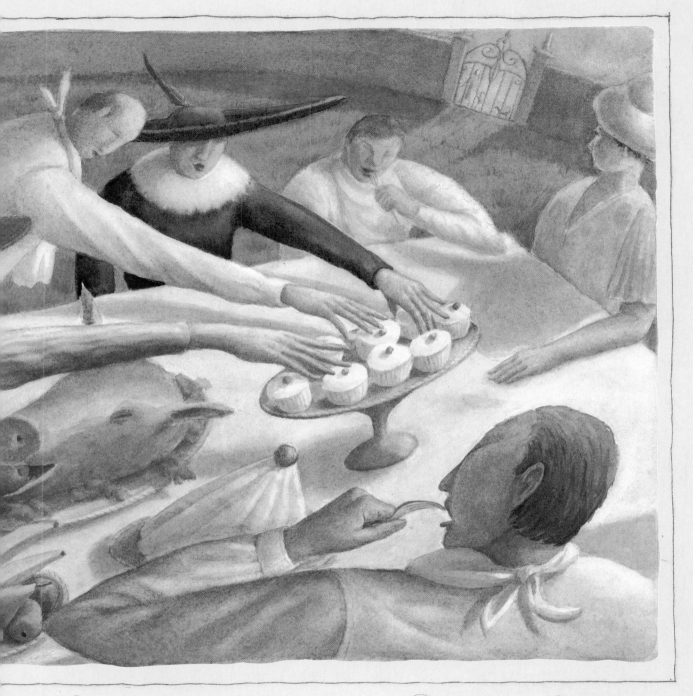

In a second, Maud had left the table. Kicking off
the pink shoes, she ran wildly over velvet lawns, past
marble statues, stately urns and shaded monuments,
out into the quiet streets.
The sun had set. The people were
all indoors. But still Maud did not stop. She ran
on blindly through the sheltering dark. Her glorious hat
was lost, her dress was dirty and torn. She did not think
of them. Her ears were full of mocking laughter and
her tired feet carried her without thought
the swiftest way to home.

Shame pursued her as she slammed the door behind her. Her own house rocked and hummed with it. And the tree in the corner stood lifeless and dead.

Maud did no fishing that night. She stripped off the ruined dress and huddled in her bed, haunted by nightmare banquets filled with greedy, gobbling faces and shrieks of cruel mirth.

In the morning she rose and went down to the shore. With her she took the remains of the dress and the pink vase with its withered plant.

All day Maud worked hard with her
needle and when her long lean boat put out
to sea, there was a sail to drive it. The setting sun was
spreading gold upon the water as she lowered her net
and waited for the fish that were her livelihood. Tired
but content, Maud watched the splendour fade.

But first, she dropped the pink vase
overboard and let it sink.

MORE WALKER PAPERBACKS
For You to Enjoy

THE TWELVE DANCING PRINCESSES
by Anne Carter / Anne Dalton

"Updated for today's younger reader without losing any of the
original atmosphere. The detailed pictures are quite charming."
Practical Parenting

0-7445-1794-X   £3.99

THE TWELVE DAYS OF CHRISTMAS
illustrated by Louise Brierley

"Outstandingly pretty and imaginative."
Country Life

0-7445-0395-7   £3.99

LOVE AND BE WISE
by Anne Carter / Jean Claverie

This classic seventeenth-century French fairy tale by Charles Perrault
tells the story of the ugly but clever Prince Riquet of the Quiff who falls
in love with the silly, but very beautiful Princess Dora.

"Witty and stylish with delicate and imaginative colour illustrations.
A treat to look at and to have read aloud or to be enjoyed alone."
Practical Parenting

0-7445-3055-5   £4.99

**Walker Paperbacks are available from most booksellers, or by post from
Walker Books Ltd, PO Box 11, Falmouth, Cornwall TR10 9EN.**

To order, send: Title, author, ISBN number and price for each book ordered, your full name and address,
cheque or postal order for the total amount, plus postage and packing:

UK and BFPO Customers – £1.00 for first book, plus 50p for the second book and plus 30p for each additional book to a maximum charge of £3.00.
Overseas and Eire Customers – £2.00 for first book, plus £1.00 for the second book and plus 50p per copy for each additional book.
Prices are correct at time of going to press, but are subject to change without notice.